The Stalker

the Deer Lake series

Summer of Change
How to be a Frog Millionaire
Who is Mel Randall, Anyway?
The Stalker
Stranded

DEER LAKE

The Stalker

K.E. Calder

Vanwell Publishing Limited
St. Catharines, Ontario

Vanwell Publishing acknowledges the financial support of the Government of Canada through the Book Publishing Industry Development Program for our publishing activities.

Vanwell Publishing Limited
P.O. Box 2131
1 Northrup Crescent
St. Catharines, ON
Canada L2R 7S2
sales@vanwell.com
1-800-661-6136

In the United States
P.O. Box 1207
Lewiston, NY
USA 14092

Produced and designed by Tea Leaf Press Inc.
www.tealeafpress.com

Cover illustration: Dave Calder
Design: Jane Lewis
Editorial: April Fast, Jane Lewis,
Heather Levigne, and Hannelore Sotzek

Printed in Canada

National Library of Canada Cataloguing in Publication

Calder, Kate, 1974-
The stalker / Kate Calder.

(Deer Lake)
ISBN 1-55068-124-9
ISSN 1702-0603

I. Title. II. Series: Deer Lake (St. Catharines, Ont.)

PS8555.A46515S83 2002 jC813'.6 C2002-901212-0
PZ7

For Cameron, Chad, and Travis.
Dream big!

Chapter 1

"The day your grandpa and I first came to Deer Lake was cold and rainy," said Grandma. She pulled the blanket tighter around her shoulders. "Your parents were just little kids at the time. We left them with their grandma and grandpa. It was just the two of us," she said to Will, Benny, and Joey.

"Earlier that day, a pole had fallen over in town. It blocked the main road to our new cottage. We were trapped on the highway for hours. By the time we were able to make it to the cottage road and down the driveway, it was dark outside. All the power was out. Just like tonight."

Grandma paused and looked at the three boys. The light from the candle lit up the bottom of her pale face.

"Beatrice Jones was the old woman who sold us this place. She was supposed to meet us here and hand over the keys. When we knocked on the door, there was no answer. So here we were, locked outside in the pouring rain. All of our stuff was in the car. We were wet all the way through to our bones.

Your grandpa knocked again. Then he tried turning the handle. To our surprise, it was unlocked! We opened the door a tiny bit and looked in. I called, 'Hello? Mrs. Jones?' But there was no answer.

Suddenly, there was a flash of lightning! We both burst inside the cottage. The door shut behind us with a bang. The shutters banged against the window. It was pitch black in the kitchen. Our hearts were pounding. Your grandpa and I could hardly see each other. Then we noticed a faint yellow light coming from the other room."

"You mean in here? In this room?" asked Joey. His eyes were wide open, and he was beginning to shake.

"Yes, it was coming from in here," said Grandma. "Your grandpa and I held hands and slowly walked to the doorway. 'Mrs. Jones?' I called out again. But the little old woman was nowhere to be seen. There was no sign of her. In fact, I have not heard from her since. I never found out what happened to her. All we heard was the rain on the roof. All we saw was the light from a little white candle. It was sitting right here, on this table."

Will felt a shudder run up his back. He pulled his hands into the arms of his sweater. The story of Beatrice Jones was well known in the town of Deer Lake. No one seemed to know why she disappeared without a trace.

Grandma continued, "Suddenly, the whole cottage shook with thunder. There was a flash of lightning. For a second, the walls were lit up with a bright white light. I saw a man standing on the other side of the screen door. 'Ted, look!' I cried. Then the room went dark again."

The boys moved closer together. They looked nervously at the door.

"A moment later, there was more thunder and a flash of lightning. The room lit up again. I screamed! But the man was not there. The doorway was empty." Grandma paused and looked at the doorway.

"Then what did you do?" asked Benny. The boys held their breath and leaned closer to hear her better.

"Well, we brought in all our stuff, unpacked it, and had some dinner," she said. She stood up, letting the blanket fall off of her shoulders and onto the floor.

"What?" said Joey.

"What about the man?" asked Will. He was fourteen years old—three years older than his twin cousins, but he was still a bit freaked out by the story.

"I figured it was just in my mind. Most scary things are," she said. There was a low humming sound and the lights came on. "Oh, good. The power is back," Grandma said. "Who wants hot chocolate?" she asked on her way to the kitchen.

"That's it?" said Will. "Who wants hot chocolate? *Agh!*" He thought there would be more to the story than that.

"That's it," said Grandma. She looked back at the boys with a smile. Then she turned and went into the kitchen.

Will's Grandma was like that. She liked to come up with stories for the three boys. This was Will's first summer up at Grandma's cottage since he was nine.

His mom had dropped him off only a few weeks ago. She was working in the city. She thought the best place for Will to spend his summer was at a cottage. That was where she had spent the summers when she was his age. Will was sure things must have been a lot different then. There weren't so many things to miss back then. Will missed TV, e-mail, and the Internet. The cottage had none of those things.

Those first few weeks at the cottage had been hard for Will. His twin cousins, Benny and Joey, were used to spending their summers up at the cottage with Grandma. They were his worst nightmare.

Benny and Joey found their own way to have fun. They were always playing jokes on him. One time, they pulled all his underwear through the little holes in his bedroom wall. Another time, they tricked him into hitting a raw egg on his own head. They made him think it was hard-boiled when it wasn't.

Benny even used his prosthetic arm to play

jokes. When Benny first met Will, he let his arm come off when Will shook it. Another time, Will got up in the morning to use the bathroom. The arm was sitting on top of the toilet. A false arm isn't really a scary thing. But finding an arm lying around the house can really scare the life out of you!

Will was getting better at dealing with the twins. He just never knew when they were for real or when they were trying to fool him.

Luckily, he didn't have to put up with them as much anymore. He was starting to meet more people his own age. Now, Will was hanging around a lot with Kyle Jordan. His parents owned a store near the edge of town called The Trading Post.

There were also the Randall sisters. Lindsay, Mel, and Sarah Randall lived in a cottage four doors down from Will. It was on the very end of Skokie Road, which was the twisty road that went around Deer Lake. When Will was nine years old, he had played with the Randall girls. That was the last time he had seen them.

This summer, he had hardly talked to the girls at all. He wasn't planning on getting to know them, either. He tried to avoid talking to girls at all costs. It wasn't that he didn't like them. He just wasn't very good at it.

Grandma's cottage was on Deer Lake in the town of Deer Lake. Will hadn't been there for years, but it was still exactly the same as he remembered. There was a rusty old swing on the front porch. A long wooden table sat in the kitchen. There was a twisty path that led from the cottage to the beach. Down at the beach was a dock. And, of course, there was still their old, grumpy neighbor, Booker.

Chapter 2

Will sat down on the wooden dock. He pulled his Game Boy out from under his shirt and looked around. He hadn't brought his Game Boy down to the dock before. The coast was clear. Everyone was out of sight. Time for some Starship! It took him about five minutes to reach the second level of the game.

He put his hand on the dock. The wood was warm from the sun beating down on it. Even at ten o'clock in the morning, it was a hot day. There wasn't a cloud in the sky. The clear water lapped against the dock. Once in a while, a boat went by, but Will hardly noticed. He was too glued to his Game Boy.

Will hung his legs over the dock. His toes dipped in the water. He was wearing his everyday clothes—his favorite blue and green bathing suit shorts and a baggy t-shirt. His dark hair lay flat against his head. He had started putting gel in it and spiking it every day like Kyle did. He hadn't bothered to do it this morning, though. He was going to go swimming later. But right now, he was starting to really build up his army in Starship.

He was just about to attack the enemy when the Game Boy slipped from his hands. Will tried to grab it. The Game Boy hit his leg and then dropped into the water with a *kerplunk*. He watched its fuzzy shape sink deeper and deeper.

"Oh, no!" Will said. Quickly, he got down on his stomach. He put his face as close as possible to the surface of the water. He could just barely make out the wobbly outline of the Game Boy under the water. There it was, lying between two large rocks at the bottom of the lake.

Will got up and looked around. A pile of sticks and branches that he had gathered last week gave him an idea. Will ran back to the beach and picked the longest stick he could find. Then he ran back to the end of the dock.

Will poked the stick into the water. The water was too deep, and the stick was too short. It was nowhere near the Game Boy. He got back on his stomach. Will put his whole arm under the water to make the stick reach farther. It was no use. It wasn't long enough. *What good would touching it with a stick do, anyway?* thought Will.

There was only one thing he could do. He would have to go in after it. He took off his t-shirt and stood with his toes sticking over the edge of the dock. It had to be at least ten feet to the bottom. One time, he had tried to touch the bottom with his feet. But he hadn't been able to sink deep enough under the water.

Will raised his arms above his head in dive position. He leaned forward, took a deep breath in, and dove head first into the water. The water was cooler than he had expected.

Will opened his eyes and swam as hard as he could toward the bottom. Everything looked fuzzy. Will looked quickly for his Game Boy. He could just barely see it on the bottom of the lake. He reached the bottom and tried to get the Game Boy, but it was caught between the rocks.

"Ugh," grunted Will. Bubbles escaped out of his mouth and rose to the surface. He yanked at the Game Boy, but he couldn't get it. His fingers kept slipping off its sides.

He dug his toes into the gunky bottom. *Yuck!* Will thought to himself as the mud oozed between his toes. He didn't usually let his feet touch the bottom.

He pulled again and the Game Boy finally came free. *Gotcha!* he thought as the rocks rolled apart.

Just then, something shiny caught Will's eye. He reached for it, but he was already starting to float back up to the surface. He couldn't hold his breath for much longer. More bubbles escaped from his mouth. He needed to take a breath right away. He looked up. He didn't know if he was going to be able to make it back to the surface.

Chapter 3

Will held the Game Boy in his right arm. He kicked his legs as hard as he could to swim back up to the dock. He reached the surface and took a big breath of air.

Will held onto the ladder. It took a moment to catch his breath. He climbed halfway up the ladder and leaned on the dock. He held out the Game Boy. Water gushed from its sides. The screen was empty.

"Oh, no!" Will yelled. He tried turning it off and then on again. Nothing. He gave it a good shake and tried all the buttons. Nothing. It was busted. His mom was going to be really mad when she found out!

He set the Game Boy down on the dock with a sigh. He couldn't believe it was broken.

Then Will remembered the shiny object he had seen on the lake bottom. He leaned to the side to look back under the water. He crouched on the ladder and put his face close to the surface. He could just barely see the small, shiny object at the bottom where his Game Boy had been.

What is it? thought Will.

He put his face in the water and opened his eyes. It looked small and fuzzy. He was too far away from it to tell what it was. He looked up at the beach, hoping to see one of the twins' snorkeling masks lying around. For once, all of the toys and snorkeling stuff were put away in the cottage.

Figures, he thought.

He looked back at the water. *Here goes,* he thought. He took a deep breath and jumped back down into the water. When he reached the bottom, he picked up the object. It was small and metal. He put it in the pocket of his bathing suit. Will pushed off the muddy lake bottom with his feet. He kicked his way back up to the surface.

Suddenly, his head hit something hard. He looked up to see what he hit, but he was in darkness. All he could see were little lines of light shining above him.

What is going on? Will thought to himself. Then he realized what had happened. He had swam up under the dock! He was trapped under water!

Oh, no! I'm dead! he thought. In a panic, he began banging under the dock with his fists. He looked straight ahead, but there was only darkness. He wasn't sure which way to swim. He couldn't hold his breath any longer.

I just have to find the edge, he thought. He used his arms to pull himself under the dock. Finally his hand felt the edge, and he ducked his head under the lip of the dock. He came up on the other side.

Will coughed as he took big breaths of air. Then he pulled his upper body up onto the wooden surface. He laid his head on the warm wood and tried to catch his breath.

No one was around. A few more seconds and he could have passed out under water. His family wouldn't have been able to find him. Will breathed a sigh of relief. *I guess this is why*

Grandma doesn't want me to go in the lake by myself, he thought.

Will reached in his pocket and pulled out the object he found under water. He dropped it on the dock and held his head up. It was a set of shiny keys on a little metal ring. Will picked up the keys. He looked back down into the water. There was nothing else down there. Then he looked back at the keys in his hand.

What could these keys be for? Will thought. They weren't Grandma's. He knew what her keys looked like. He wondered who could have lost a set of keys in front of his cottage.

What if they were Beatrice Jones' keys? He quickly pulled himself out of the water and onto the dock. One of the keys was small and silver with a round top. It looked like it could be for a small lock, like the small lock a chest.

A chest! Maybe Beatrice Jones was locked in a chest. That would explain her disappearance. That would also explain the fact that no one knew where she was. Will imagined himself finding the chest. He would use the key to open it. The lock would be rusty and hard to open. He would slowly lift open the lid and…

"What are you looking at?" said a voice behind Will, making him jump.

"Stop scaring me!" Will said. Why were people around here always scaring him out of his wits? "Nothing…just fish," he said angrily and slipped the keys into his pocket.

"There are fish down there? Cool," said Joey. He sat down beside Will to look at the water. Sometimes Joey could be so rotten. Other times, like right now, he just seemed like an okay kid.

"I don't see any fish—hey, what happened?" he said and picked up the Game Boy. Water streamed out of its side and onto the dock.

"Uh, I dropped it in the water," said Will. He had forgot about his Game Boy.

"That sucks!" said Joey.

"Yeah, it does," Will said.

"Are you going to tell your Mom about it?" Joey asked.

"No," said Will.

"Good call," said Joey. "Hey can I have this?" he asked pointing to the Game Boy.

"What for?" Will asked.

"I just want it," he said.

"Take it. Knock yourself out," said Will. He couldn't figure out why Joey wanted a busted-up Game Boy, but the kid was weird. There was no doubt about it.

Will got up. He left Joey sitting on the edge of the dock with the Game Boy. He reached in his pocket and pulled out the keys. Will had a lot of locks to try.

Chapter 4

Will ran across the beach and up the dirt path to the wooden cottage. Its brown paint was peeling in spots. Some of the screens on the closed-in back porch were ripped.

Instead of running up the back steps to the porch, Will went under them.. He opened the door that led to the space under the cottage. The cottage was built on a hill. One side of the cottage was propped up on thick beams. Boards were nailed to the beams around the outside to form walls.

Will looked around the space. Sunlight streamed in through the cracks. This was where Grandma stored old and unused cottage things. An old canoe, some battered paddles, and a set of wooden water skis sat on the dirt ground. Water toys, flippers, snorkels, and fishing rods leaned up against the walls.

It was a creepy place, but Will was used to it. When he first arrived at the cottage, he came in here to hide frogs. For a few weeks, Will ran his own frog-catching business. He had caught a lot of them. He sold the frogs to Bud's Bait shop in Deer Lake. After a while, Will gave up the frog business. He found out that if he caught too many frogs, the frog population might die off.

Will looked around the room. *I know I've seen a padlock on something in here,* he thought. He just couldn't remember where.

Will looked around. There was an old kitchen cupboard leaning up against one of the beams. Then he saw it—the padlock! It was on a chain holding the cupboard doors tightly shut.

All of a sudden, Will's throat felt dry. The cupboard was pretty big. Big enough to hold a whole person. Will didn't want to think about what could be behind those doors. He pictured Beatrice Jones' cold, dead body stuffed inside the cupboard.

This was worse than he had thought. Beatrice had been right under their noses the whole time. How many times had he come down here for a fishing rod or an old beach chair? *And the whole time, a dead little old lady was just ten feet away,* he thought.

Will gulped and walked over to the cupboard. He held the keys tightly in his hand. He tried to put the first key in the padlock. It didn't fit. Then he tried the second key in the padlock. It fit the lock, but it wouldn't unlock it. It just wasn't the right key.

I guess I've got the wrong lock, thought Will, giving the lock a tug. The metal padlock opened! The rust had worn it away over time. Now it was open. Will slowly took the padlock off the chain. He pulled out the chain. It banged loudly against the handles of the cupboard door. With both hands on either handle, Will slowly opened the doors. Keeping his eyes shut, he thought, *Here goes.*

Will turned his face to the side and slowly opened his eyes. The cupboard was empty except for a cobweb and a bunch of dust balls.

"What are you doing?" said a loud voice behind him.

Chapter 5

"Ahhhh!" Will yelled and turned around. "I told you not to do that," said Will.

"Not to do what?" his cousin said. He was standing in the doorway.

"Scare me," said Will.

"No, you didn't," the twin argued.

"Yes, I did," Will said.

"When?"

"Just a minute ago, Joey, down at the—" he stopped. It was Benny standing there, not Joey. Sometimes, Will couldn't tell the twins apart. "Never mind. Just don't scare me like that," Will said.

"What's in there?" asked Benny.

"Nothing, actually."

"Uh-huh," said Benny. He wasn't interested in what Will was doing. Then he quickly turned around and walked out. The wooden door closed behind him.

Bye-bye, thought Will.

Will knew for a fact that the twins were scared to go under the cottage. Of course, they never said so to him. Will could tell by the scared looks on their faces whenever they went near it. In fact, they never went farther than the doorway. Will knew exactly where to go to get away from the twins. The space under the cottage was the perfect escape!

Will waited for a few seconds after Benny left. Quietly, he went out the door. He watched Benny walk down to the dock where Joey was playing with the broken Game Boy. Then Will slipped quietly up the steps to the porch.

One by one, he tried all the locks in and around the cottage. He tried the back door to the cottage and the padlock on the trash bin. He tried the lock on the old window frame, even though it was always left open. None of them were a fit. He even tried the keys in the lock on Grandma's car. No luck.

It was just a stupid, old set of keys that someone had thrown away. Will got out of the car and pushed the door shut. Then he walked gloomily across the lawn. He sat on the porch swing at the front of the cottage.

Will wondered what his friends back in the city were doing right now. Some of them were at their summer jobs. The rest of them were probably hanging out at the food court at the mall. Will felt like he was missing out on all the fun his friends were having. They would all be talking about their summer adventures when he got back. What would he tell them? He'd feel like a little kid if all he could tell them was that he found an old set of keys. Oh, and that he had caught a bunch of frogs.

"Hey, Willy," said Joey from behind the screen door to the cottage.

"What do you want?" said Will. He had given up on trying to get them to not call him Willy. They just did it even more when he asked them not to.

"Do you want to play Starship?" Joey asked him.

"On what?" asked Will.

"Our new Game Boy," said Joey.

"You mean *my* Game Boy, and it's broken," said Will and rolled his eyes.

"You gave it away, so it's ours now. Besides, we dried it out and it works," said Joey and held up the game.

"What? Let me see," said Will. He got up, but Joey quickly shut the door in front of Will. Will heard a click from the inside. He tried to open the door, but the little brats had locked him out.

"Hey, let me in," shouted Will into the wooden door.

"Not by the hair of our chinny, chin, chins," said one of the twins. They both laughed on the other side of the door.

"Very funny," said Will. Then he remembered the keys. It was worth a try. He put the first key in the lock and wiggled it, but the lock didn't open. He put the second key in the lock. It worked! The key slipped in the lock and turned with a click. "Aha!" Will said as he opened the door.

Benny and Joey stopped laughing and turned to look at Will with shock. "Let's get out of here," yelled Benny. They both ran out of the kitchen as fast as they could.

Will didn't bother following them. He had bigger things to think about. He pulled the keys out of the lock and turned them over in his hand. So they *were* Beatrice Jones's old keys after all. But what were they doing in the lake? And why had she vanished?

Chapter 6

Will heard a door bang shut. He looked out the kitchen window. Booker, his grumpy, old neighbor was coming out of his cottage. He was wearing a red-checkered jacket and beige shorts. He wore dark green socks that were pulled up almost to his knees and brown leather shoes. His gray hair was sticking out from the bottom of his fishing hat.

Booker lived in the cottage next door. He had been there for years. No one ever really talked to him. Once in a while, Grandma said "hi" to him if they were putting out their trash at the same time. Most times he would just grunt and walk away.

Booker just didn't seem interested in talking to his neighbors. In fact, he didn't even seem interested in talking to anyone. Grandma said she didn't want to bug him if he didn't want to be bugged.

"Some people just like to be left alone," Grandma said.

Grandma didn't know much about him. Well, she knew his name wasn't really Booker. It was Alfred Zwicker. Most people didn't even know that, though. Will had only ever heard people call him Booker.

The old man often went to the library to borrow books. He also went to the little used bookstore in town. He liked books, and that was all anyone really knew about him.

Kids whispered with fright and ran away when they saw Booker. They giggled when they passed by him in town. Weird people like Booker were the kind of stuff that town tales were made of.

Booker got into his big, old car. He began backing slowly out of his driveway. *He must be going into town,* Will thought.

All of a sudden, Will remembered Grandma's scary story. A strange man had been standing in the doorway of the cottage. Could it have been Booker? Maybe he didn't want to be bugged for a reason. Maybe he was hiding something.

What if Booker knew what had happened to Beatrice Jones? What if he really had murdered her? Will imagined Grandma on the evening news.

"He was just a quiet man who kept to himself," he pictured her saying to the reporter. That's what people always said when they found out that their next-door neighbors were murderers.

Will decided it was time to look around for clues at Booker's place. He waited until Booker's car had gone down Skokie Road. He watched it go around the bend. Then Will made his move.

Will ran through the trees and bushes between the cottages. Booker's cottage was silent. Will looked around. No one was watching. He had the set of keys he had found in his pocket. He crept onto Booker's porch and tried a key in the lock. It didn't fit.

Will didn't have much time to waste. Booker could return at any time. He ran to the other side of the cottage and found a side door. He tried the key again. He wiggled it in the lock but it didn't work there either.

Will returned to the front of the cottage. He saw two large wooden doors. They were almost flat against the ground beside the cottage. They looked old and worn.

They must lead to some sort of a cellar under Booker's cottage, thought Will. *Just the sort of place to hide a body.*

He tried the small key in the padlock on the cellar doors. He jiggled it, but it didn't work there, either. Will sighed.

He walked around to the other side of the cottage. There was just one more lock to try. The garage. The garage was not attached to the cottage. It was an old, shabby building beside the driveway. The paint had worn off long ago.

There were small dirty windows on one side of the garage. Will couldn't see inside. The windows were too high. Even if he could reach them, they were probably too dirty to see through them anyway. On the front of the garage was a huge blue door. It was large enough for a car to drive through. Beside it was a regular door.

Will tried the key in the padlock on the large door. It didn't fit at all. He took a deep breath. This was his last chance. He put the key in the other door. It turned the lock. He was in!

Will pushed on the door. It hardly moved. *There must be something on the other side,* he figured. He pushed harder. Whatever was on the other side moved a little.

Just then, Will heard the sound of tires on the road at the end of the driveway. He stopped moving. He saw the front end of Booker's car turn into the driveway. *Oh, no!* Will thought. *What if Booker sees me looking around on his property?*

Will pushed with all his might. The door opened just enough for him to wiggle inside. He shut the door again and sat down with his back against it. His heart was beating a mile a minute. He tried not to breathe too loudly.

Will heard Booker's car come to a stop. The car door slammed shut. Will heard the sound of Booker's footsteps on the driveway. He was walking closer to the shed. Will held his breath.

Booker's footsteps passed by the garage door. They got quieter as he moved away. Now Booker was walking up the steps to the porch.

The cottage door opened and then shut as the old man went inside.

Man, that was close! Will thought.

He put his hand down beside him and looked down. He had been so scared of Booker finding him that he hadn't noticed was what he was sitting on. It was big, black bag. A body bag! "Ahh!!!!" yelled Will. He jumped off the bag, tripped onto the floor, and quickly leapt to his feet again. He had found the body!

Chapter 7

Will slowly put one foot behind the other. He backed away from the body. His arms and neck had goose bumps, and his entire body was trembling with fear.

"I don't believe this," Will said out loud. His chin began to shake. He was taking short, quick breaths. His mouth was hanging open, and his eyes were wide and glassy.

He hadn't even looked around the room yet. What else was hidden in here? Terrified, Will looked from side to side. The inside of the garage was smaller than he had thought. It smelled musty too. There was just a bunch of old boxes, a toolbox, and a dead body.

Faint light came through the small, dirty windows. Will spotted a broken broom handle leaning up against the wall. He picked it up and held the long handle straight out toward the body. Will inched a little closer to it. Slowly, he made his way across the floor.

The tip of the handle was close enough to the body to touch it. Will held his breath and gently poked the cloth bag.

It wasn't hard like Will had thought a dead body would be. He poked it again. The stick made a mark in the bag's shape. He moved the handle to the far right side of the bag and poked there. The same thing happened. He walked closer and stood over the bag. Then he lifted his foot and placed it on the bag. It didn't feel like a body.

Will bent down near the opening. Slowly, he lifted the edge of the bag and peered inside. The bag was full of little stacks of paper or cardboard. Will reached in and pulled out one of them. It was a pack of hockey cards tied with a rubber band. He reached in and pulled out more little packs of hockey cards. It was an entire body-sized sack filled with hockey cards. Will couldn't believe it!

He took a closer look at one of the packs. They were old hockey cards. They were *really* old—from the seventies. Hockey players with funny haircuts. They were wearing old-fashioned uniforms. Their skates looked really ancient. *What the…?* thought Will. He couldn't believe it. Hockey cards. He had been scared of hockey cards!

Will put the cards back into the bag except for one pack. He put it in his pocket. He wanted to look through them later on. Maybe he could figure out why someone would want to keep them. Beside, Booker had a whole bag full of them.

Will stood up and pressed his ear to the door. He couldn't hear anyone walking around. Will pulled the door open a tiny bit and peeked out. Booker must have gone inside the cottage, but Will couldn't tell for sure. He pulled the door open far enough to stick his head out and look from side to side. Booker was nowhere in sight.

Quickly, Will pulled the door open. When he stepped outside, he put his foot right in the mud. He pulled out his foot, but his shoe was stuck in the mud!

He heard Booker's screen door swing open and bang shut. He didn't want Booker to see him walking around his place, shoe or no shoe. Will sneaked across Booker's driveway. He ran through the bushes and trees and back to his own cottage with one shoe and one bare foot.

Chapter 8

That night, Will could hardly eat dinner. He couldn't stop thinking about the keys and Booker's garage. Why would Booker's garage key be with Beatrice's house key? What was Booker hiding? Did he murder Beatrice Jones?

"Earth to Willy," said Benny. He waved a hot dog in front of Will.

"Huh?" said Will. He wasn't even bothered by those two tonight. He had more important things on his mind.

Grandma also noticed the way Will was acting. "Will, what's wrong with you?" she asked him.

"Nothing," he said.

"You've hardly touched your hot dog. And you haven't eaten any macaroni and cheese. It's your favorite," she said.

Will looked down at his plate. His macaroni and cheese was cold and clumpy.

"Do you want me to reheat that for you?" Grandma asked him.

"No, I don't mind it cold," he said. He jabbed his fork in the mound of macaroni and pulled out an orange clump. "Can I have some ketchup?" he asked. Grandma handed him the big plastic bottle of ketchup. Will squeezed the last bit of ketchup onto his macaroni with loud, messy squirts.

"Do you miss your mother?" Grandma said. She looked worried.

"No. I mean, yes. But I'm fine. Okay?" He couldn't tell her about finding the keys. Then he would have to tell her that he had gone onto Booker's property. She would be mad for sure. He couldn't tell her that he thought Booker might be a murderer, either. She would never believe him.

"Okay, okay," Grandma said. "I was just wondering why you're so deep in thought," she said.

That night, Will went downstairs to brush his teeth to get ready for bed. When he was finished, he headed back up the stairs.

"Good night, Willy," called Joey from the twins' bedroom as Will passed by.

"Hmph," said Will. He went into his dark bedroom and closed the door. He couldn't stop thinking about Beatrice Jones. What if Booker had murdered her in *this* cottage? What if she was haunting the place?

He lifted up the covers and crawled into bed. Just as he was laying his head down, he felt something hard on his back. He flipped over onto his stomach and poked his hand in the covers. His hand felt another hand. It had cold, smooth fingers.

"Ahhhhh!" Will yelled and jumped out of bed. He ran over to the door and turned on the light. It took a second for his eyes to get used to the bright light. He let out another yell. There was an arm lying in his bed! He took a closer look. It was an arm all right—Benny's arm.

"Hey! Benny!" yelled Will. The door opened a crack.

Benny poked his head around the corner. "Yes?" he said.

"Very funny," said Will.

"What?" he said. Benny pretended not to notice the arm lying in Will's bed. "Oh, *there* it is," he said. "I've been looking all over the place for it."

Will could hear Joey giggling in the next room. Benny slid by Will and walked over to the bed. He picked up his arm and attached it to his elbow.

"Thanks, dude," he said and walked past Will and out the door. "Good night."

Will just rolled his eyes and got back into his bed.

Chapter 9

The next day, Will had one thing on his mind—Booker. He had to get to the bottom of the mystery keys. The twins had gone into town with Grandma. Will had the cottage to himself. This was a perfect time to keep a close eye on Booker. Will could watch him and find out what he was up to.

There was a cupboard behind the big orange chair in the living room. Old board games, torn books, and a brown recorder were piled on top of it. Will climbed on the chair and reached over it. He pulled open the drawer.

Carefully, he lifted a pair of binoculars out of the drawer. He had just seen Grandma put them in there the night before. She had taken them out to look at a little yellow bird in a tree. He knew Grandma would be upset if anything happened to them. *I'd better be careful with these,* Will thought.

Where will be the best place to watch Booker? Will wondered. He went to the back porch and crouched down below the screened windows. He leaned on the ledge and looked out in the direction of Booker's cottage.

Will raised the binoculars to his face and peered through them. Leaves. All he could see were leaves and branches. *This is no use. I'm going to have to get a lot closer,* he thought. *I bet I'd have a better view if I watched Booker's cottage from the beach.*

Will hung the binoculars around his neck. He went down the back steps to the path that led to the beach. He crouched behind the bushes at the edge of the path just before the beach. If only he could make it to the water and watch Booker from there. Then he could crouch down beside the dock to keep from being seen.

How the heck am I going to get across the beach without Booker seeing me? he thought. He crept onto the beach and lay down on his chest. The binoculars hung down his back. Slowly, he squirmed across the sand on his stomach. Will spotted Joey's air mattress lying by a lawn chair. He put it over his back for cover.

Will held onto the sides of the air mattress on either side of his head. It was long enough to cover his entire body from head to foot.

Slowly, he inched forward. He used his elbows to pull himself along the sandy beach. If anyone saw him, he hoped it would just look like an air mattress being blown across the beach. He inched farther on the sand.

Finally, he reached the dock. Will crouched down behind it so Booker would not be able to see him. He let go of the air mattress and crawled toward the water on his hands and knees. He peered over the dock and brought the binoculars around to his front.

Safe, he thought.

From his new lookout, Will could see everything. He raised the binoculars up to his face and peered through them. He could everything close-up. He pointed the binoculars down to the water. There was Booker's dock and the path that led up to his cottage. There were the steps that led up to his porch. Will raised his hands and looked along the porch. There he was! Booker!

Through the metal screen door, he could see Booker. Will could only see him from the shoulders up, though. He figured Booker must be sitting down. Booker was looking down at something. Maybe he was sewing a body bag! Or maybe he was just reading.

Will stared at Booker through the binoculars for a long time. He was sure Booker would make a move any minute now. Will's arms were getting tired. Booker just kept on sitting in his chair. He sat and sat and sat. He hardly moved at all.

Will put down his binoculars and looked around. There was no one in sight. Good.

He turned back to Booker's cottage. He peered at the same spot on the porch where Booker was sitting. He wasn't there. Will couldn't see Booker's head and shoulders.

Shoot, I lost him, thought Will. He moved the binoculars slowly to the side and looked along the porch. Booker's big orange cat was sitting on the railing, licking its paws. Will reached the end of the porch through the binoculars. *Where the heck is he?* Will thought. He looked along the other direction.

Cat…empty chair…more empty porch… Booker…Booker! Will jumped. Booker was standing up and looking out through the screen. Will had a close-up view of Booker's face looking right at him.

Chapter 10

Will jerked his head back from the binoculars. Quickly, he ducked his head down behind the dock and turned around. *Oh, no! Did he see me?* thought Will. His heart was still pounding. *I guess I'm trapped here until he stops looking,* he thought. Booker would see him cross the beach if he tried to leave.

Will stayed crouched behind the dock. He'd just have to wait until he was sure that Booker wasn't spying on Will spying on him. Will sat down on the wet sand. As long as he was here, he may as well get comfortable.

The sun was beginning to peek through the big, puffy white clouds. Will reached into the water and picked up a stone. It was light orange and completely smooth. He flicked it, and it skipped across the water a couple of times. Skipping stones was one of those things that looked a lot harder than it really was.

He'd seen Benny skipping stones the other day using his prosthetic arm. Will tried not to stare at Benny's arm all the time, but he couldn't help it. Benny could do everything that everyone else could do. Even with that arm. It didn't take Will long to realize that he didn't need to feel sorry for Benny. He thought about all the jokes that Benny and Joey had played on Will.

Will looked across the lake. He could see a little white spot on the far shoreline. He lifted up his binoculars. It was a sailboat. Someone was washing it.

Suddenly, a big blue object was right in front of him. Will put down the binoculars. A canoe had moved in front of his view of the sailboat. It was on this side of the lake. It wasn't right in front of him, though. It was actually just at the edge of his bay.

He raised his binoculars again. It was a light blue canoe with a metal rim. He looked farther along until he could see who was paddling it.

Mel Randall!

Will moved the binoculars along to see the back of the canoe. There was a dark-haired girl with Mel. Will had never seen her before. He pointed the binoculars to the front of the canoe again to take another look at Mel. He watched her paddle.

He hadn't seen this Mel close-up before. Well, not since he was a little kid, anyway. Mel's shoulder-length light brown hair was tied back in a braid. She was wearing a purple bathing suit and jean shorts. She had hemp bracelets on her arms.

She and the other girl were talking. Their voices carried across the water, so he could hear what they were saying. He could also see their mouths moving through the binoculars. Will could make out what they were saying.

"Hey, Allison. Remember that guy I was talking about?" said Mel.

So the other girl is called Allison. Good to know, thought Will.

"Yeah, did you see him the other day?" said Allison.

"Yeah. He was in town when I was there. He didn't see me, though. He is so cute," said Mel as she dipped her oar in the water.

This was interesting. *Who are they talking about?* he wondered.

"What was he doing?" asked Allison.

"He was just walking out of the ice cream shop," said Mel.

"Why didn't you say something?"

"Are you nuts? I can't just walk up to him and start talking," said Mel.

Hey! Will thought. *I was in the ice cream shop a couple of days ago! Does Mel Randall think I'm cute? Me, cute?*

He hadn't been called cute since he was seven years old and was a bear for Halloween. *Hmmm, Will Bergeron, cute guy,* he thought to himself. He knew that spiking his hair was a good idea.

Wait a minute. They have to be talking about someone else. No girls are ever afraid to talk to me, Will thought. If anything, *he* was afraid to talk to girls.

"Why didn't you say something to him?" asked Allison.

"What would I say? 'Hi, I think you're

cu—'" she stopped just as she looked toward Will's cottage. Will quickly put down his binoculars. He tried to hide them behind his back. Mel was looking right at him. The canoe wasn't very far away from him at all now.

"Hi," Mel called. Will raised his hand and gave a little wave. Mel looked at him for a moment and then looked back at Allison. They giggled and kept on paddling. The canoe went past his cottage and around the point to the next bay. Will raised his binoculars again. He watched the back tip of the canoe disappear behind the rocks.

Girls, thought Will.

Then he remembered why he was sitting there in the first place. Booker. He turned around and faced Booker's cottage. Slowly, Will raised his eyes above the dock. He couldn't see Booker. He must have gone inside his cottage.

Will jumped up and raced across the beach to the path. He had to follow Booker. But wondering whether or not he was cute was going to bug him all day.

Just then, Will heard a car door bang shut. The sound came from Booker's driveway. Will ran up the path and around the side of his cottage to see where Booker was going.

He crept into the bushes between their driveway and Booker's. Through the trees, Will could see Booker. He was dragging a huge sack like the one Will had seen in his garage. He lifted it up into his trunk and slammed it shut. Then he got into his car and backed down the driveway.

What was that? Maybe that was the sack that Beatrice Jones was in. Maybe he had filled the other one with cards to fool people. All along he had been hiding a body. Where was he going with it?

One way or another, Will was going to find out the truth.

Chapter 11

Spying on Booker was not going to be easy. Will couldn't drive. He couldn't follow Booker into town or wherever he went in his car. Will needed more clues.

Maybe there were more clues at the bottom of the lake. If Booker had thrown keys into the water, who knows what else he might have thrown in.

While Will was deep in thought, Benny wandered into the kitchen.

"Hey, uh, Benny," said Will

"What?" said Benny. He opened the cupboard. Benny stood there looking at the food inside.

"Can I borrow your snorkeling mask?" asked Will. He pretended to read a magazine on the table. Will didn't want to sound like he really wanted it.

"No way! I don't even let Joey borrow my snorkeling mask," said Benny.

Just then, Grandma walked into the kitchen. She was wearing a long, baggy dress. It had huge bright pink, blue, red, orange, and yellow flowers on it. Will and Benny just stared at her. Sometimes, she wore strange things like this and Will wondered what she was thinking.

"Do you guys like my muumuu? I got it in Hawaii with your Grandpa. I thought I had lost it," she said. She held out the sides of the dress. The muumuu spread almost two feet out on both sides. It was hard to look at her without laughing. Will and Benny didn't say anything. "So, what's going on in here?" she asked.

"I was just asking Benny if I could borrow his snorkeling mask," said Will. He looked at Benny. He knew that with Grandma there, Benny would have to say yes. After all, it was a perfectly nice question.

It was a tricky move. He'd probably pay for it later, but Will really needed that mask. He was willing to pay the price. Grandma looked at Benny, waiting for his answer.

"Yeah, sure," Benny said slowly. "It's out on the back porch behind the life jackets." Benny looked at Will with narrowed eyes. Grandma glanced at him, and he instantly changed his face to a smile.

"Thanks," said Will.

"No problem, Willy," said Benny. Willy. Benny knew that Will hated when they called him Willy. It was Benny's way of saying, "you won't get away with this!"

Chapter 12

The mask made a sucking noise as Will pushed it onto his face. He put the snorkel in his mouth. It smelled and tasted like rubber.

He walked into the water. He had to walk with big steps in the flippers he was wearing. They slapped on the water with each step. Then he floated on his stomach and put his face in the water. Will began kicking his feet. The flippers moved him forward quickly.

The water was very clear. Will could see everything on the bottom. Wet brown leaves covered the muddy bottom. Every so often, there was a big rock. A couple of times, he saw little fish. They swam away quickly as he got closer to them. The only thing he could hear was the sound of his own breathing through his snorkel.

Will stopped swimming and raised his head out of the water. He looked back at his cottage. He had swam far from his beach. He was now swimming in front of Booker's cottage. The mystery area. Will put his head back down in the water and swam farther. Leaves, stick, soda bottle, a little fish.

Bonk!

Will jerked his head out the water. He had bonked his head on something. Will ripped off his mask. Booker was right in front of him! He was wearing a snorkeling mask, too. Will had bonked heads with Booker.

"Ahhhhh!" Will yelled.

Will turned around. He swam with his arms churning through the water, back toward his own beach.

"Hey, come back here!" called Booker. Will just kept on swimming as fast as he could. He reached the water in front of his beach. His knees hit the sandy bottom. Will stood up and tried to run to the shore. His flippers tripped him, and he fell on his face in the water. He splashed to the shore on his hands and knees as fast as he could. He ripped off the flippers and dropped them on the sand. Then he ran across the beach. He ran up the porch steps, through the cottage, and into the kitchen.

"Will, you are all wet!" said Grandma.

Will stood beside the table. His heart was pounding. His bathing suit was dripping a steady stream on the floor. His mask and snorkel were hanging under his chin. He tried to talk, but he couldn't catch his breath.

"I…snorkeling…heads…Booker…," he said between breaths.

"Will, calm down," said Grandma. She walked over to him and put her hands on his arms. "Now take a deep breath. That's good. Now what seems to be the problem?" she said.

"I was snorkeling," Will burst out.

"Yes, and…?" Grandma waited for Will to finish his story.

"I bonked heads," he said. "With Booker." He blew a big breath out of his mouth.

"And?" said Grandma, still looking at him with concern.

"I swam away as fast as I could," said Will.

"And?" said Grandma.

"And then I ran up here," said Will.

Grandma dropped her hands and looked at him.

"So what's the matter?" she said.

"Booker was snorkeling too," said Will.

"He always snorkels," she said. "Haven't you ever seen him out there before? You can see his snorkel moving back and forth in the water. He usually goes in front of his cottage," she said.

Aha! So he always snorkels right in front of his own cottage, thought Will. *He must be looking for something.* Now Will was sure that there was something down there. But what? Maybe it was more keys. Or maybe it was the chest with Beatrice Jones's body!

"Yeah, right. I knew that," said Will, trying to play it cool. He didn't want to alarm his Grandma. She didn't know there was a murderer living right next door.

Chapter 13

Will had to tell someone about Booker. He couldn't tell the twins. They couldn't be trusted. There was only one person Will knew who might know something.

"Can I go into town for a little while?" Will asked his Grandma.

Will was walking up toward Kyle Jordan's house just as Kyle and his mom were driving up in their car.

"Hey, dude," said Kyle, sticking his head out the car window. His dark hair was spiked. It had chunks of light blond highlights on the tips. The car stopped, and he got out. Kyle was wearing a bright green t-shirt and a wet suit.

The top of the wet suit was open and folded down around his hips.

"Good timing, dude. I just got off work." Kyle said. He worked a lot at his family's store, The Trading Post. It was on the highway just outside of Deer Lake on the other side of town. The Jordans sold everything from groceries to sandals to water skis.

"Do you want to hang out?" asked Will.

"Yeah, cool. Hey, you can be my spotter. We just got this new wet suit in, and I want to try it out," said Kyle.

Kyle wakeboarded every chance he got. If he wasn't working at the store, you could bet that he was wakeboarding. He always needed a spotter to sit in the back of the boat. It was the spotter's job to tell the driver if the person on the wakeboard fell. Kyle hardly ever fell, though. He was one of the best wakeboarders on Deer Lake.

Will followed him around the cottage and onto the back porch, which faced the lake.

"Do you guys want lunch?" Kyle's mom called from inside the cottage.

"Yes, please," they both yelled back at the same time.

"You have to see this trick I just learned yesterday," said Kyle. "It's a heelside back roll flip. I don't think any of the other guys can beat it," he said. Kyle was getting ready for Wakefest. It was an awesome wakeboarding contest that took place on Deer Lake.

Will didn't really know what a heelside back roll flip was. He knew it was some sort of wakeboarding move. He guessed Kyle would flip up and turn upside down in the air.

Kyle made wakeboarding look easy. *How hard can it be?* Will had thought the first and only time he had tried it. *It's just like water-skiing, but on a board.* Seven wipeouts later, Will had given up. Wakeboarding was a lot harder than it looked.

"Sounds great. Hey, does your family know Booker? You know, the old man who has a cottage beside mine?" asked Will.

"Yeah, dude, everybody knows about him."

"Do your parents know anything about him?" said Will.

"Yeah, he's weird," said Kyle. He was wiping off his wakeboard. "I'm so glad I got this new board. No one else at Wakefest will have anything this cool," he said.

"Did your family know Beatrice Jones?" asked Will. "She used to live in my cottage about thirty years ago."

"I've never heard of her," said Kyle. He picked up his life jacket. "Agh, it's not dry yet. I hate putting on a wet life jacket," said Kyle. He shook the jacket over the deck. He wasn't interested in Booker or Beatrice Jones.

"Hey, do you want to go first?" he asked.

"No, not today," said Will. *Not after the last time,* he thought. He was going to stick to waterskiing.

"I think Booker is hiding something," said Will. He was hoping that Kyle would be willing to help him spy on Booker.

"Who?" said Kyle.

"Booker, our neighbor," said Will.

"Hiding what?" said Kyle.

"A dead body," said Will.

Kyle stopped drying his life jacket and looked at Will. Finally, Will had his attention.

"What?" said Kyle.

"A dead body," said Will.

"What?!"

"I think he killed Beatrice Jones," said Will.

"Why do you think that?" asked Kyle.

"Because, she disappeared without a trace just before my grandparents moved into the cottage," said Will.

"Dude, there's no way he could hide a dead body for thirty years. She would just be a bunch of bones by now," said Kyle.

Will hadn't thought of that. "But…well… maybe he hid the bones somewhere. And if he killed her, he might have killed other people," said Will.

"Yeah, right," Kyle said. Will could tell he didn't believe him. "Is the rope over there? Maybe it's in the boat," he said. "Mom, can I go wakeboarding before we eat?" he yelled.

"Okay," Mrs. Jordan yelled back.

Will sat in the back of the boat and watched Kyle wakeboard. As usual, Kyle didn't fall once. After they got back to the dock, Will didn't stay for lunch after all. He didn't feel like listening to Kyle talk about his wakeboarding moves all day. He liked Kyle, but he didn't like wakeboarding as much as Kyle did. Will said good-bye to Kyle and to Mrs. Jordan.

"Dude, don't forget Wakefest. It's this Saturday," said Kyle.

"Yeah, I'll be there," said Will with a long face. He really was looking forward to Wakefest. He just wished that Kyle believed that Booker was a murderer.

"It's going to be awesome!" said Kyle.

Chapter 14

On his way home, Will passed the hardware store. He looked at the fishing rods leaning up against the window. "SALE! 30% OFF," was painted in big red letters on the glass.

Will looked at each rod carefully. He hadn't fished a lot this summer. Not as much as he had fished last summer at sleepover camp. So far he had only caught a big slimy bunch of weeds and a few sunfish. Grandma's fishing tackle was pretty old. Some of it had been his Grandpa's. If he had the right rod, maybe he could catch something worth keeping.

Just then, something caught Will's eye inside the store. Will peered through the letters on the glass. A gray-haired man walked past the window. Will looked closer. He knew that red-checkered jacket anywhere. Booker! He leaned toward the window and peered in at Booker. What was *he* doing here? What was he buying in the hardware store? Just then, Booker started turning toward him.

Quickly, Will ducked below the window. He got on his hands and knees. He peeked over the edge of the window. He could see Booker walking through the store. Then, Booker picked something up and started walking toward the cash register. His back was to the window, but Will could see what he was buying. Booker set a long rope up on the counter. And an ax!

Will gulped loudly. A chill ran down his back. Booker was buying some rope and an ax! Two must-have things for any killer. Will's heart was pounding. What was he going to do with it? Who was his next victim?

After Booker paid for his "supplies," he walked toward the front door. Will crawled on his hands and knees along the sidewalk to the side of the hardware store. He crouched down around the corner, out of sight. He got there just in time. Booker came out of the hardware store and headed toward his car.

Will peeked carefully around the corner. He saw Booker open his trunk. The blade of the ax gleamed in the sunlight as he set it in the trunk along with the rope. Will watched him get in his car, back out of his parking space, and drive away.

Chapter 15

Will spent the next few days spying on Booker. He stalked him every minute of the day. When Booker went down to fix his dock, Will went down to the beach. He pretended to read or make a sand castle while he kept an eye on Booker. When Booker went into his garage, Will hid in the bushes between their driveways. And when Booker went into his house, Will spied on him from his spot down by the dock.

One day, Will heard loud noises coming from Booker's porch. It sounded like he was chopping wood and banging a hammer. What was he building? A large box perhaps? Maybe something big enough to bury his next victim in. Or maybe he was ripping up the floor boards of his porch. Maybe Beatrice Jones' bones were hidden under the floor! Will couldn't be sure.

That night, Will crept downstairs to get a drink of water. As he stood at the sink, he saw something outside the kitchen window. It looked like a little ball of light. It was moving in the trees near Booker's cottage. Will put his head to the window. He cupped his hands around his face so he could see better into the darkness. The moving light was from a flashlight. Then Will saw him. Booker seemed to be looking for something in the dark.

Maybe he's looking for the spot where her bones are buried, thought Will. T*hat was a long time ago. Maybe he can't quite remember where he buried them.* Then Booker went back inside his cottage. Will waited to see if Booker would come back outside, but he didn't. Will went back up to bed. He slept with the light on for the rest of the night.

On Thursday morning, Will was sitting on the front deck. He had the binoculars pointed at Booker's cottage.

"Will!" said Grandma "Stop staring at Booker's cottage. You can't spy on people like that. I don't know what you think you're going to see, anyway," she said.

"I think Booker is up to something," said Will. He raised his eyebrows.

"Up to what?" said Grandma. She looked at Will and shook her head.

"I can't say," said Will.

"What do you mean 'you can't say?'" said Grandma.

"You wouldn't believe me," said Will.

"Try me," said Grandma.

"I think Booker is a murderer, and he's hiding a dead body."

"I don't believe you." She thought it was silly. Will could tell.

"See?" he said, shaking his head.

"That's silly," said Grandma. "Booker has been our neighbor for years."

"Yes, but what do we actually know about him?" said Will.

"Plenty," she said. Will could tell she didn't want to talk about Booker anymore.

"I'm taking Benny and Joey to the public beach in town. We're going to watch Wakefest.

Are you coming?" she said, changing the subject. Will decided he could use a break from spying on Booker.

"Okay," said Will. "I'll be ready to go in five minutes."

The twins were already dressed in their best skater-style t-shirts and baggy pants. Benny had a bright blue cap on sideways.

"Yo, Willy," said Joey. "Are you going to show us your wakeboarding moves today?" he asked. Joey pretended to lose his balance on a wakeboard. He fell onto the grass.

"Yeah, we want to see you get some air, dude," said Benny.

"Kind of like the air between your ears?" said Will.

"Oooooh, that hurt, Will. That cut deep," joked Benny as they all piled into the car. Will was starting to get used to trading insults with the twins. Making fun of each other had become a game for him, too.

All three boys were eager to go to Wakefest. Will had never been to a wakeboarding event. Wakefest was being held at the Deer Lake public beach at the far end of town.

Chapter 16

The parking lot was packed with cars and vans when they arrived. A huge banner said "Welcome to Wakefest." Teenagers walked in among the cars. They leaned on their cars and sat in the back of their pickup trucks.

Grandma's brown car rolled through the parking lot. Will saw some of the other kids. Now he was sorry that he hadn't picked out some cooler clothes to wear. Somehow he felt a little boring in his usual beige shorts and plain blue t-shirt. Everyone at Wakefest was wearing brightly colored shorts and t-shirts. Will wished he had a cool hat or a pair of wakeboarding shorts.

There were tons of girls Will had never seen before. A lot of them were just wearing bikini tops and shorts. He quickly looked over the crowds. Mel and her friend were nowhere in sight. He didn't know why, but he hated the thought of trying to talk to her. It was dumb. She was just a girl his age, but he didn't know what to say. He didn't want to say something lame and look a like a loser in front of her.

Will saw wakeboards and bicycles leaning against fences and cars. Bathing suits and t-shirts hung from windows and tree branches. Music blared through big speakers set up by the beach. A huge truck was parked at the entrance to the beach. "CKLB HITZ 103" was painted on the side of the truck.

"Awesome. CKLB HITZ 103 is here!" said Joey. "I'm going to ask them to play a song." Grandma pulled into a parking spot. Joey had the door open as soon as the car came to a stop.

"Wait. Hold on a minute, guys. Don't go running off just yet. It's noon now. Don't you want lunch first?" asked Grandma. She fixed the huge brown sunglasses on her face.

Oh, no, Will thought. It was bad enough he had to walk through the parking lot with his

Grandma. Would he have to hang out with her and the twins for the whole day, too?

"Here is fifteen dollars for each of you. That should be enough for some lunch, a drink, and snacks later on," she said. She counted out the money. Will couldn't believe it. He was free for the day!

Benny and Joey put the money in their huge pockets and jumped out of the car. They raced through the parking lot and went straight to the radio station van.

"Thanks, Grandma," said Will.

"You're welcome," she said. She waved her hands at Will. "Go on. Shoo."

Will walked through the parking lot. He went past the radio station van. He came to a huge grassy area that sloped down to the water. Blankets were scattered on the grass. People were eating fries and burgers. The salty scent of the fries drifted up to him.

He decided to go over to the food stand. A lot of kids were bopping their heads to the beat of the music. He walked past the CKLB HITZ 103 van. He could feel the beat of the music in his chest. He could smell the suntan oil as he walked by groups of people tanning on blankets. Will spotted the food stand to the far left of the grassy area. He went over to get some fries for lunch.

As he waited in line for his fries, a guy's voice called from behind him. "I don't suppose you have chicken wraps here?"

"No, just burgers and fries and whatever else is on the board," said the girl in the stand. She pointed up at the big white board with black lettering behind her.

"It figures," said the voice.

Will turned around. It was that jerk Will had seen with Mel at the movie a few weeks ago. Will had seen the guy once before that, too. He had run straight at Will's canoe with his huge speedboat. He had almost tipped Will's canoe. Will was sure the guy thought it was really funny.

There was Mel. She was standing right beside jerk-boy and looking at Will. And they were holding hands! Will tried not to stare. He looked to the side and then looked over his shoulder. He felt silly standing right there in front of them. Will wanted to just walk away, but he couldn't. He was waiting for his fries.

"Uh...hi," he said.

"Hi," said Mel.

"I guess we'll take two orders of fries then," jerk-boy said to the girl behind the stand. Ted noticed Will standing in front of them. He was just about to say something to Will when the girl in the stand yelled "Fries!" Will took the white cardboard box of fries. He walked away as smoothly as he could.

"Don't you want ketchup?" yelled the girl.

"No, thanks," called Will without turning to look back. What was Mel doing with that guy? Chicken wraps? Who did he think he was? Was that the kind of guy she thought was cool? If that was the case, what did she really think of Will?

Chapter 17

Will walked down to get a good view of the water. The wakeboarding contest was starting. A guy who looked a bit older than Will was ripping back and forth over the wake. The music blared loudly down by the water.

A man's voice boomed over the loudspeakers. "That was a fine toeside tail grab! Brent just needs to get in some more tricks to bring up his score," said the voice. The wakeboarder took off over the wake. He did a back roll flip with a handle pass. The bottom of his board gleamed as it arced above his upside-down body. He landed hard, but he held on and jumped back over the wake.

"All right, let's hear it for Tony Brent and that cool handle pass!" The crowd on the grass cheered. Will found an empty patch of grass. He sat among the other kids to eat his fries. He wished he had taken that ketchup or maybe some salt. They tasted kind of plain without anything on them.

One after the other, the wakeboarders took their turn on the water. They flipped, turned, and jumped over the wake behind the boat. Some of them did major wipe outs. The kids around Will yelled out the names of the wakeboarders they knew. People clapped and cheered at the tricks. Even Will started to cheer and yell. It was cool when someone landed a really huge jump.

Everyone was having a great time. On the dock, the wakeboarders waited for their turn. Some of them danced around to the music that was playing. Groups of kids flocked down to the water to get the wakeboarders to sign their t-shirts. Some of them had their pictures taken with them.

"Next up is Deer Lake's own Kyle Jordan. He is using a brand-new O'Brien board from The Trading Post." said the voice over the loudspeaker. The crowd on the grass went wild. Everybody knew who Kyle was.

"Oh, it's him. Come on, I want to sit here so we can get a good view," Will heard a girl say. She plopped herself down beside Will. He rolled his eyes.

She must be one of Kyle's fans, he thought. He turned to look at who it was. It was Mel's friend, Allison. She was the one he had seen in the canoe with Mel. Mel sat down beside her. Will looked around for jerk-boy, but he wasn't with them. Mel saw Will at the same time that he saw her.

"Hi," she said.

Will quickly turned back toward the water and kept his eyes on Kyle. The boat took off. Kyle skimmed over the water.

"Oh, hi," he said, keeping his eyes on Kyle. *Stay cool. Stay cool. She's just an old neighbor. You played with her when she was a little kid,* he thought to himself. Mel's friend Allison gave her a swat. She cleared her throat really loudly to get her attention.

"This is Allison," said Mel.

"Hi," said Will. He quickly turned his head for a second to say hi. Then he turned his head back to the water so quickly he hardly even saw her face.

The crowd yelled and clapped for Kyle. He did trick after trick on his wakeboard. Kyle wrapped the handle behind his back. Then he popped into a full back roll flip and turned his body in the air.

"Did you see that? He just did a wrapped back roll," said Allison.

"Yeah, that was pretty cool," said Mel.

"I'm *so* going to meet him when he gets back to the dock," said Allison. "Hey, you know Kyle Jordan, right?" she asked Will and poked his arm.

"Yeah," said Will.

"Could I come with you to meet him?" Allison asked.

"Yeah, I guess," said Will.

"Cool," said Allison. Will turned back to the water. Great, now he had to take her over to say hi to Kyle. How did he get himself into this? They watched Kyle move back over the wake to get ready for his next trick.

"So, where is your boyfriend?" Will blurted out to Mel. She looked surprised. He wished he hadn't said it. He didn't even know where it had come from. He could feel the back of his throat going dry.

"If you mean Ted, he's gone back to his cottage. He wanted to get some bottled water. He's coming back," said Mel.

"Oh," Will said.

"Hey, Will, don't you wakeboard?" said Allison.

What was he supposed to say? He had wakeboarded, but he could hardly say that it was a hobby of his. In fact, he could hardly get out of the water. He water-skied, but everybody on Deer lake water-skied. That was hardly anything great.

"I had my own frog business," said Will.

Just then Kyle did some great trick on his board. The crowd went wild. The cheering drowned out Will's voice.

"What?" Both of the girls looked at Will with surprise.

"I said, I used to catch frogs," yelled Will. By this time the crowd had stopped cheering. Some people around them turned to look at him when he yelled.

"Oh." Both of the girls just stared at Will with funny looks on their faces. Then Allison turned to bury her face in Mel's shoulder. Will could hear her making a gagging noise as she tried not to laugh. Mel just stared at him with a weird grin. Will looked out towards the water. He could feel his neck and face getting hot. He knew he was turning bright red.

Out on the water, Kyle was finishing his turn. He stepped off his wakeboard and did a handstand on the dock. Everyone cheered. A huge group of kids ran toward the dock with their cameras.

Chapter 18

"So, did everyone have fun at Wakefest?" asked Grandma. She put a steaming hot cob of corn on Will's plate.

"Yeah, it was so awesome," said Benny. "I even got Tony Brent to sign my shirt," he said. He turned around in his seat. He showed off the name written on the back of his t-shirt in blue marker.

"Wow, I hope that was written with a waterproof pen," said Grandma. She plopped a steaming cob in front of Benny.

Will tried to spread some butter on his corn, but it just kept sliding off. "Just roll it right in the butter, dear," said Grandma. She rolled her cob of corn in the butter on the table. It made a deep, corn-shaped mark. His mother would have never let him do that at home.

"Will was hanging around with girls," said Joey. He plopped his corn in the butter.

"I was not," said Will.

"Yeah, you were. We saw you. You were talking to Mel Randall and the new girl," said Benny. He grinned.

Will just wanted to forget about that. He felt like an idiot. He wished he hadn't told the girls about his frog business.

"So what?" said Will. He wasn't going to let these fools tease him about talking to a girl. After all, he was fourteen. He was supposed to be talking to girls.

That night, Will lay in bed thinking about Wakefest. He was going to have to get better at wakeboarding. He was also going to have to learn not to blurt out things like, "I used to catch frogs." He felt dumb just thinking about it. Maybe the girls would forget that he had even said it.

Will shut his eyes tight. He imagined himself doing a handstand on the dock and the crowd cheering.

It was the middle of the night when Will opened his eyes. He must have drifted off to sleep. Will lifted his head and peered out his bedroom window. Everything outside was still. He heard a sound. He looked into the darkness of his room. He couldn't see a thing.

He put his head back down and closed his eyes. It was an old cottage and it was always making sounds in the middle of the night. There was nothing to worry about.

Then he heard another louder sound. It sounded like the door downstairs. He sat up in bed and held his breath. Then he looked out his bedroom window again. The front screen door of the cottage was swaying open. Someone was breaking into the cottage!

He hoped he was wrong. He hoped it was nothing. Then Will heard a loud rustling coming from downstairs.

Booker! Who else would break into the cottage? He must want his keys back. *I bet he's searching the cottage for them, Will* thought. Will flipped back his covers. He crept out of his room and into the dark hallway.

The rustling sounds were getting closer and closer to the stairs. There was another noise. Then something landed with a bang on the bottom step.

"Grandmaaaaaaaaaa!" Will yelled from his bedroom door. He heard something moving downstairs. The front door flew open and banged shut again. Grandma came running out of her bedroom and into the hall. The light came on in Benny and Joey's bedroom.

"What? What? What is the matter?" cried Grandma. Her eyes were only half open.

"What's going on?" said Benny. Both twins came out into the hallway.

"Booker was in here!" said Will loudly. "He just left when I called you. Booker broke into our cottage."

"Will, for Pete's sake! Booker is not breaking into our cottage. What has got into you? Go back to bed," she said angrily.

"He did. He was downstairs. I heard him," said Will pointing down the steps. The twins stood there quietly, looking a bit scared.

"I'm going downstairs to check just so you'll go to bed," she said. She marched down the stairs. The three boys followed.

Of course, there was nothing downstairs. He hadn't seen him, but Will knew what he had heard. Booker had been tip-toeing around outside in the dark the other night. This time he had been in their cottage. There was no doubt about it.

Will left on his light for the rest of the night. Every little sound made him jump. He didn't fall sleep until four o'clock in the morning.

The next day, Will went straight to the porch. He was completely glued to the binoculars. He stared and stared at Booker's cottage. The old man only came out once to pick up an armful of firewood. *He's in hiding,* thought Will. *He knows that I'm on to him.*

"Will, stop that," said Grandma after dinner. Will was still looking through the binoculars. He had hardly moved from the porch all day.

"I don't know why you have it in your head that Booker is some sort of bad person. He did not break into our cottage. I'm going to prove it to you," she said. Will wondered how she could possibly do that.

Grandma went into the kitchen and came out with a big bag of flour.

"What is that for?" said Will.

"You'll see," she said. She reached into the

bag and took out a handful of flour. She sprinkled it all over the floor.

"What are you doing?" asked Will.

"You'll see," she said. "Come with me." Will followed her around to the front door of the cottage. She sprinkled more flour on the front steps. She even sprinkled it inside the door on the rug. Will was couldn't believe it. He knew his Grandma was a bit weird sometimes, but this was nuts. Maybe Booker was like a vampire. Only instead of sunlight, he couldn't go near flour.

That night, Will slept with his light on again. He lay awake for hours, listening for Booker to break in. Finally he fell asleep.

Chapter 19

"Will, come down here and see this," yelled Grandma from the bottom of the stairs. Will opened his eyes. He was so tired, but he couldn't wait to see what was downstairs. Would Booker be lying in the flour?

Will ran downstairs. Grandma and the twins were standing around the front door. "Look at Booker's footprints," said Benny, and he looked at Joey. They both laughed.

Will looked at the floor. There were tiny paw prints in the flour. The paw prints continued as little white marks on the rug. The little prints zig-zagged all over the kitchen and out the back door.

"What made those prints?" said Will, rubbing his eyes.

"Raccoons," said Grandma. "We've had trouble with raccoons for years. Somehow they got in through the screen door." Will couldn't believe it. *Raccoons?* That would explain the rustling sounds he had heard. But he had been so sure that it was Booker.

Maybe raccoons had broken into the cottage. But that didn't explain everything. No amount of tiny paw prints could change the facts. Will saw Booker stuff a body bag into his trunk. There was also the rope and ax that Booker bought in the hardware store. And there was that day that Booker was snorkeling. Will was sure he was searching for something in the water.

Will had to prove that Booker was a murderer. Who would he go after next?

After breakfast, Will decided it was time to look for more clues. He was going over to Booker's garage to see what else he could find. But first he had to get the twins off his back.

"Hey Willy, do you want to go into town with us?" said Joey.

"No," said Will.

"But you know Bud from Bud's Bait. We want him to show us the tanks of eels in the back room," said Benny.

"Tough, ask him yourself," said Will.

"We'll let you play our Game Boy if you come," said Joey.

"It's my Game Boy, and I can play it whenever I want," said Will.

"It *was* your Game Boy, until you gave it away," said Benny.

"That's because I thought it was broken. It's still mine. I'm taking it back at the end of the summer," said Will.

"That's what you think," said Joey.

"Agh!" Will said. He walked out the front door, shaking his hands in the air.

"Hey, where are you going?" Benny called.

"Nowhere!" said Will. He didn't look back. He went around to the side of the cottage and stopped. He listened. He wanted to make sure that the twins weren't following him. He didn't hear anything.

Will crept quickly across his driveway. He went through the bushes and trees to Booker's driveway. He looked around. The coast was clear. Booker was nowhere in sight. Will pushed back the branches he was standing behind. He ran across Booker's driveway to his garage. He ran around to the side.

There was all sorts of junk piled at the side of the garage. Will saw a huge stack of wood, shovels, rakes, and buckets. He also saw two very large wooden boxes. He would have to go through it all carefully for clues.

Will walked over to the woodpile and picked up a piece of wood. Several other pieces of wood knocked to the ground. Will stood still for a moment. Then he looked around the corner of the garage to see if anyone had heard the noise. There was no one there.

He went over to one of the large wooden boxes. It was shut tightly with a screw. Will tried to unscrew the nut. It was covered in rust. He wiggled it, but it wouldn't turn.

Just then, Will heard a branch snap. He stopped what he was doing and stood very still. He heard another branch snap. He knew it—Benny and Joey had followed him to Booker's cottage.

"You guys go home," he said without turning around. He kept trying to loosen the screw. He didn't hear anything. They were probably still there, spying on him. He started to turn around.

"I said, get out of here—"

A big hand took Will's arm. He was face to face with Booker! "I caught you in the act!" Booker said. Will didn't move. He had never been so scared in his life. He could hardly breathe. "You're coming with me," said Booker. He held on to Will's arm with his huge hand. He pulled Will across the driveway and back through the brush. The branches slapped Will as Booker dragged him through the trees and bushes.

"Grandmaaaaaaa! Help!" Will yelled as they stepped onto Will's driveway. He kept yelling until Booker put his hand over Will's mouth.

"You don't need to yell bloody murder," said Booker. *Bloody? Murder?* That made Will yell even more. But only a gagged sound came out from behind Booker's hand.

Chapter 20

"Mr. Zwicker! What on earth is going on out here?" said Grandma. She walked quickly down the porch steps. Booker took his hand off Will's mouth. He let go of Will's arm. Will ran over to his Grandma. The twins came out of the cottage and stood quietly on the porch.

"Your little grandson here is a thief," said Booker, pointing at Will.

"He is trying to murder me. He knows that *I* know that he murdered Beatrice Jones," said Will. He pointed at Booker.

"What? *You've* been breaking into my garage. I found your shoe in the mud. You've got my spare keys. I know you do. I saw your footprints going into my garage. I need those keys back so that I can go through my collection," said Booker.

"You just don't want me finding any clues," said Will.

"I want those keys back. They're mine," said Booker.

"Then what were they doing at the bottom of the lake?" Will asked him.

"I lost them weeks ago. I've been searching for them every day," said Booker.

"Everyone calm down," said Grandma with an angry voice. "Will, did you find Mr. Zwicker's keys?"

"They aren't Booker's keys, they were Beatrice Jones's keys. They open this cottage," said Will. "He threw them into the lake himself when he murdered her."

"There is a spare key for my garage on that key ring," said Booker. "And what do you mean, *'when I murdered her?'*"

"I'm sorry, Mr. Zwicker. Will has been cooking up a story for a couple of weeks now. He thinks you are a murderer," Grandma said. She shook her head at Will.

"WHAT? I just want my garage key. I have

to sort through my hockey cards. There is a card dealer in the city. He says he's interested in buying the whole collection," said Booker.

He leaned forward and put his hands on his knees. He rubbed his hand across his head and then across his thin gray beard. All of a sudden, Booker didn't look so scary and mean anymore. He just looked like an old guy.

"Will, is this true? Have you been breaking into Booker's garage?" asked Grandma.

"Well, just the one time," said Will.

"'Just the one time?!' Well, once is quite enough," said Grandma.

"But…those are Beatrice Jones's keys," said Will in a quiet voice.

"Yes, of course they are," said Booker. "I kept a set of spare keys for her. She had a spare set for me, too. We were neighbors for years and years, you know." He sighed and paused for a moment.

"I kept them in my tackle box. One day, when I was going fishing, the lid opened as I was getting into the boat. The keys fell into the water," said Booker.

"Is that why you've been snorkeling almost every day?" asked Grandma.

"Yes! I lost my regular set of keys and I needed the spare. I haven't been able to get into my garage," Booker replied.

"Why didn't you ask me, Mr. Zwicker? Beatrice left me an extra set of spare keys, you know. I have one for your cottage and garage," said Grandma.

"What? Well, I'll be! Beatrice left in such a hurry. I didn't figure she had taken the time to do that," he said.

"Yeah, right," said Will. He wasn't buying this story. He wasn't about to be fooled. "Where did she go in such a hurry?"

"Sunnyview, the old age home. Didn't you folks know that?" he asked with a surprised look on his face.

"No," said Grandma. She seemed even more surprised.

"Her grandchildren helped her pack up her things," said Booker. "They took her there when she sold this place. She was sad to leave, but she was having a hard time getting around by herself. Beatrice wanted to move quickly into Sunnyview, where people could take care of her."

"We had no idea what had happened to

her," said Grandma. "She didn't leave a note for us or anything."

"Yes, she did. I remember. She taped it to the front door," said Booker.

"Well, it must have blown off in that terrible storm," said Grandma.

"But what about all that banging and cutting you've been doing on your porch?" asked Will. "And why were you outside with a flashlight in the middle of the night?" Ha! How was Booker going to explain *that*?

"Those darn raccoons. They've had me up almost every night. I've tried to go after them and scare them away. I even built a trap. I had to cut the wood and hammer it together myself," Booker said.

All of a sudden, Will felt kind of silly.

"Mr. Zwicker, why don't you come in for some tea? I think it's about time we got to know each other better," Grandma said. She motioned for Booker to follow her up the steps.

"Okay, but please call me Alfred. We've been neighbors for a long time. You don't have to call me Mr. Zwicker," he said. He followed Grandma into the cottage.

Chapter 21

The twins backed up and sat on the deck chairs as Grandma and Booker passed them on the porch.

"We're out of here," whispered Benny to Will. They took off down to the beach. Grandma poked her head from behind the screen door.

"Will, come in and have some tea with us," she said. Will walked into the kitchen.

"There is something I need to get first. I'll be right back," he said. He went up to his room and looked under the mattress. He pulled out the stack of hockey cards that he had taken from Booker's garage. He went back downstairs. Booker was sitting at the table and Grandma was filling up the teapot.

"I guess I should give you these back," said Will. He handed the cards over to Booker.

"Thank you," said Booker. He flipped through the stack. "I haven't looked at these in a long time," he said. He looked at Will. "Tell you what. You can keep these ones. I've got a whole garage full of them." He handed the stack back to Will.

"Gee, thanks," said Will. He didn't really want a bunch of old hockey cards. He flipped through the pile.

"Those are collector's cards," said Booker.

"That's good," said Will. He still didn't understand why people would collect old stuff like this.

"That stack is probably worth a couple hundred dollars," said Booker. Will's eyes lit up. *A couple hundred dollars!*

"Really? Thanks!" he said. Booker and Grandma laughed. Then Grandma stopped laughing. She her hand over her mouth.

"Oh dear," Grandma said and looked at Will and then Booker. "I think I may have started this murder idea of Will's." She folded her hands together and looked down to her side. "I told Will and the twins a scary story. It was about the day that my husband and I moved into the cottage. I think I may have created a monster."

"There was no monster in that story, Grandma," said Will.

"What I mean is, I think I planted a thought in your head. It grew out of control," she said to Will. Then she turned to Booker. "There was a thunder storm that day and the power was out. By the time we got here, Beatrice Jones had already left," said Grandma.

"Yes, I remember the day," said Booker.

"I might have gotten carried away just a bit. I love a good scary story. And besides, it's a true story." she said.

"Speaking of true stories, do you know about the row boat that sank out past the end of the point?" Booker asked.

"No," said Grandma.

"There was a young couple on board. The man had taken the woman out for a ride in the boat. It was just over in the next bay. He wanted to ask her to marry him under the full moon. The boat is still down at the bottom of the lake somewhere," said Booker. "On nights when there is a full moon, people say they can hear sounds coming from the point. They say they can hear splashing and choking sounds."

Will felt a chill go up his back. He sat down at the table beside Booker.

Grandma sat down too.

"Go on," she said.

Glossary

back roll flip with a handle pass
A wakeboarding trick

binoculars
A handheld tool that is used to look at objects that are far away

cottage
A small house that is used for vacation

heelside back roll flip
A wakeboarding trick

hemp
A type of plant that is used to make rope or cloth

macaroni
A short, tube-shaped noodle

muumuu
A long, loose Hawaiian dress with bright colors and patterns

recorder
A musical instrument that looks like a flute

picnic
A meal that is eaten outdoors

prosthetic
Describing a false body part, such as an arm or a leg

snorkel
(noun) A tube through which a person breathes while swimming underwater; (verb) to swim underwater while breathing through a tube

stalker
A person who follows and watches the activities of another person

tackle
Fishing gear, such as lures

toeside tail grab
A wakeboarding trick

vampire
A dead person who is said to rise from the grave and drink the blood of sleeping persons

wakeboard
(noun) A long, flat board used for the sport of wakeboarding

wakeboarding
A water sport in which a person stands on a board and is pulled by a boat. He or she performs tricks while being towed by the boat.

waterskiing
A water sport in which a person is pulled behind a boat while on skis

wet suit
A tight suit worn for water sports to help keep the body warm

wrapped back roll
A wakeboarding trick

Read more about

Mel Randall, Will Bergeron,

and Deer Lake

at

www.tealeafpress.com

Special Thanks

Tea Leaf Press gratefully acknowledges the help of educators Gary Osmond, Kerri Wall-Wilson and Ingrid Krahn for volunteering their time and providing invaluable insight.

Many thanks to those who took the time to read the manuscript and give us feedback—Mitchell Cox, Leslie Perry, and Megan Voth.

Also, we wish to extend our gratitude to our partners and families for their generous support and assistance. Thank you to Sam Turton, John Evoy, Ron Fast, Peter Hough and Ursula Sotzek.

Finally, we wish to extend our most sincere thanks to Ben Kooter and Vanwell Publishing for the opportunity to make our dream become a reality.